I AM SKYE, FINDER OF THE LOST

I AM SKYE, FINDER OF THE LOST

Catherine Stier

illustrated by
Francesca Rosa

Albert Whitman & Company
Chicago, Illinois

With much appreciation to the volunteer canine search and rescue teams for their dedication to finding the missing, the injured, and the lost—CS

To our trip to America, for it filled our life with everlasting memories—FR

Library of Congress Cataloging-in-Publication data
is on file with the publisher.

Illustrations by Francesca Rosa
First published in the United States of America
in 2021 by Albert Whitman & Company
ISBN 978-0-8075-1677-5 (hardcover)
ISBN 978-0-8075-1681-2 (ebook)

Printed in the United States of America
10 9 8 7 6 5 4 3 2 1 LB 24 23 22 21 20

Design by Valerie Hernández

For more information about Albert Whitman & Company,
visit our website at www.albertwhitman.com.

Contents

Chapter 1

Ready to Run

"Ready to go, Skye?" my favorite human, Susan, says in a high-pitched, cheerful voice. She knows my answer is always the same.

You're doggone right I am!

She opens the covered back of her truck, and I bound happily into my doggy car bed.

Soon we're motoring along, and I'm looking out the back window. There's so much to see!

RESCUE

I watch as the morning sun paints the bushes, trees, and hills of the Mojave Desert with yellow light.

At a big brown sign, we take a turn.

Hey, I recognize this road, I think. My nose twitches with excitement.

Before long, our truck pulls up next to a small building. A person wearing a ranger hat and badge waves us through. We're regulars here, Susan and me. We visit this desert park almost every week.

I know the desert trees that grow here, with their crooked limbs and sticky-out leaves. I know about the desert tortoises and the rattlesnakes that hide among the rocks. I know the smells of all the growing things, and the sand and the stone.

And I know what we'll be doing here today.

Our truck stops outside an old ranger station, and I see that our teammates have already arrived. The humans—Christopher, Marisol, and RJ—are all wearing matching sweatshirts, just like Susan's. We dogs have matching vests. There's a bloodhound named Bear, a standard poodle named Birdie, and Pilot, a golden retriever. And me? I'm a border collie and the newest member of the group.

We're all part of the park's volunteer canine search and rescue team. We're here to train so that we'll know how to help find people who are lost or hurt in the California desert. Bear, Birdie, and Pilot are already certified search and rescue dogs. They each passed a test and got a certificate. I'm not there yet. But I'm learning!

While the humans discuss plans for this

morning's training session, we dogs greet each other with friendly sniffs.

"Can we start Skye off with a puppy runaway?" Susan asks. "She's already raring to go."

I get to go first today? Sweet! I think.

I'm excited now, but the first time I heard about "puppy runaway," I thought there was a problem—like maybe a dog had run off and gotten lost. It wasn't that at all. It's really a fun game of hide-and-seek!

To start today's game, Susan gently holds my collar while Christopher, Bear's human partner, trots down the road. I watch Christopher go around a bend in the road and duck behind some desert plants.

Christopher, you're not very good at hiding, I think. *I saw exactly where you went!*

Susan lets go of my collar. "Search," she says.

She doesn't have to say it twice! I love the feeling of the breeze ruffling through my fur as I run. In no time, I round the bend and am nose to nose with Christopher, who is crouching in the dust. I turn tail and run back to Susan. I paw at the ground twice. That's my signal that lets her know I've made a find.

When Susan says "show me," I take off again, with her following at my heels. I bolt down the road and proudly lead her right back to Christopher.

At the sight of me, Christopher pops up, and both he and Susan cheer like it's a big party and I'm the doggy guest of honor. I wriggle with happiness and gobble down a treat.

Okay, I admit it. This first game, this puppy runaway—it's pretty easy-peasy stuff. But it's a blast! Everyone is always so excited when I find the hiding human.

Still, I know this game is just a warm-up for the bigger training challenge, the one that really tests my skills. The one that shows if I am truly cut out for search and rescue work.

And that challenge? It's coming next.

Chapter 2
High and Low

Before we start the next game, Susan flips open my doggy dish and pours water into it. Puppy runaway is thirsty work! When I've had my fill, Susan flattens the bowl and attaches it on a hook she calls a *carabiner*, which hangs from the backpack that she tosses into the truck.

Then Susan snaps a long leash onto my collar. "Skye and I are about to run the trailing exercise. Will you be the flanker?" she asks Christopher, and he nods.

"Marisol has already headed out to lay a trail," Susan continues. "And she gave me this." Susan holds up a bag with a sock inside. She makes

a funny face and laughs. "Marisol promised me she got it good and stinky jogging yesterday."

Susan opens the bag and says "get scent." I know just what to do. I stick my nose inside and snuffle up a great big whiff of Marisol's sock. I don't know why Susan made that scrunched-up face. Smells okay to me!

How can I describe the scent? The sock smells like only a human can, of course. Yet there are bits of scent that make it different from every other human—a special scent that could only belong to one human. The human I'm supposed to find.

Once I am done sniffing, Susan says, "Got it? Search!"

This game is much harder than puppy runaway. I didn't watch Marisol run off and hide. Instead, I have to find her by remembering the scent in the bag and matching it to a scent I can pick up in the air. That isn't always easy.

I raise my nose, searching for a whiff of the right smell.

I turn my face to one side, and then another.

No, not this way, I think. *No, not here... Wait! There it is!*

My tail wags, and I'm off with my nose pointed toward the ground. Maybe most humans don't know this, but all people shed tiny skin flakes wherever they go. We dogs, with our superpowered noses, can smell those bits of skin. Trailing dogs like me learn to follow that scent.

On windy days, those skin flakes can blow around or get caught in the brush. That's why trailing can be so tricky. But even though a breeze is stirring things up today, I'm determined to find Marisol and win this game.

I start in the direction of the scent, but Susan holds back.

"I was just sure Marisol would have gone the other way," she tells Christopher. Then she sighs. "But you know what experts say about working with a search and rescue dog."

"That we shouldn't get in the way of the dog based on our own hunches," Christopher answers.

"That's right," says Susan. "It's just that during that training run last month, Skye ended up following the wrong trail."

"I remember," says Christopher. "She's made real progress lately, though, hasn't she?"

Susan nods.

I remember that day too. I was trailing a person's scent but lost it. As I chased around, trying to find it, I smelled other humans. I got so excited! I followed those smells instead, right to a group of people painting outside in the desert. I sure surprised those artists when I barged in—and disappointed Susan. This time, I know I'll do better.

"Okay, Skye," Susan says. "Let's see if you're on the right track."

I take off again. For a while, I'm able to home in on the scent. It's leading me through the park toward a cluster of rocky hills. Once or twice, the scent fades. I have to sniff around till I capture it again.

I'm so focused on the hunt, I jump when Christopher yells out, "Cholla cactus, left!"

I hadn't even seen that! I think as I skirt around the prickly little plant. I'm glad we have a flanker like Christopher to keep an eye out

for dangers and distractions. Those cacti can be painful on the paws!

I keep following my nose. It's leading me toward the base of the rocky hills. I'm picking up scent in the air and on the dirt, rocks, and plants along the way—and it's getting stronger. I know I'm closing in! I trot faster and hear the sound of Susan's and Christopher's boots crunching on the gravelly dirt behind me.

Finally, I reach a boulder where the scent is strongest of all. But...no one's there! I didn't mess up; I'm sure of it. Where is she?

"Hellooooo, Skye!" Marisol suddenly calls

out. I look up as she steps down from atop the boulder.

There you are! I think. *I knew you were here somewhere!*

Susan and Christopher catch up, and everyone hoots and hollers in celebration.

I happily turn from one human to the

other, wagging my tail.

See, Susan, I'm getting the hang of this! I got it right this time! I think as I gobble down the treat she gives me.

There's nothing I like better than running through the park with a purpose and then having a party like this afterward. Still, I know finding someone lost in the desert is serious business.

I can't help wondering if Susan and I will ever be part of a *real* rescue mission.

Chapter 3

Happy Helper

At midday, after the other dogs and humans have played their own hide-and-seek games, Susan and I pack up. Usually, my mood gets as prickly as a cactus and I'm as jumpy as a jack-rabbit when I've got nothing to do. But after a busy morning of training, I don't mind taking a breather during our drive home.

Home. I'm glad I have a home now with Susan.

Things were a bit rough when I was a pup. Before Susan adopted me, I lived with a human couple with two cats. Those humans stayed away from their apartment most of the day and lots of evenings too. I got restless. Sometimes, that got me into trouble.

"Oh, Skye, what have you done?" they'd say when they got home. But how did I know that a couch wasn't just a big chew toy? Or that toilet paper shouldn't be pulled from the roll and dragged all over the house?

Then there was the time I corralled the couple's cats into the laundry room. Those kitties were not happy about it. What can I say? Herding comes naturally to me! It's what Susan calls my *natural instinct*.

One day the two humans brought me to the animal shelter. Luckily, Susan found me there that same week and took me home. She loved me right away. I could see it in her eyes. Plus, she understood my restlessness.

"Skye," she told me. "I think maybe you'd be happiest with a job." And she was right.

I didn't start off in search and rescue though.

Susan first introduced me to another career, one I still work at now.

Yep, that's right. Doing search and rescue work will be my *second* job. My first job is what humans call a *therapy dog* or a *crisis-response dog*. At first, I didn't really know what that meant. Then Susan and I did some training.

"Human and dog crisis-response teams meet with people of all ages after a tragedy, like a fire or tornado," a trainer explained. "These dogs can even help firefighters and paramedics deal with stress and sadness. How do they do those amazing things? Just by sitting near a person, being friendly and calm, and offering a listening ear."

I can do those things! I thought.

To get me ready for therapy work, Susan brought me to the farmers market, the city park,

and other places to see how I got along with people and other dogs. I loved those outings—the longs walks, the fresh air, the nice people and dogs we met. All that time outdoors suited a busy pooch like me just fine.

Susan also taught me some commands. But the thing that mattered most for the job was something called my *temperament*. "Skye seems to have just the right temperament to be a therapy dog," the trainer told Susan after he met me. "She's confident and friendly. And from what I can tell, Skye loves to be around people."

Well, that last part is true enough!

I have to admit, though, that even I'm surprised that a ball of energy like me can be calm and cuddly when worried people need me. I guess having a purpose makes me happy. I never seem to get in trouble anymore!

Some folks say therapy dogs are like lie detectors. Even when someone tries to hide their sadness or nervousness, we can sense it. For dogs like me, that's easy-peasy. Honestly, humans just smell different when they're upset.

One of the best parts of my job is meeting with people during happy times too. Sometimes Susan and I go to fun places like schools or health fairs. She talks about the work we do, then invites everyone to come meet me. That part is pretty great. Susan even has trading cards with my picture on them that she gives away.

I remember during one classroom visit, a little boy came up to me. He pulled out my trading card and held it up. I could tell it was old and that he'd kept it for a while. The card was worn with bent corners and smudged with a little soot.

"Hi, Skye. I'm Jamie," the boy said. "You don't know me. But you met my dad during last year's wildfire. He's a firefighter. He said you made him feel better when he was tired and sad. He got this when he met you." The boy held the trading card close to my face. "My dad gave it to me after the fire, when he got home safely. I've kept it all this time."

Then the boy hugged me. "Thank you for helping my dad, Skye," he said. "You are a very special doggy."

You know how I said dogs can tell when humans are sad or nervous? Well, we know when humans are glad and thankful too. And it's those moments that make me most proud of what I do.

Skye

Chapter 4

Duty Calls

After my busy training morning with Susan, I'm happy to be relaxing at home. I nap a bit, but soon I'm full of pep again.

First, I explore the backyard. Then I come back inside to nose my ball around the house. I'm thinking about what to do next when Susan gets a phone call.

That call changes *everything*.

I see the serious look on Susan's face. "Okay, we're on our way," she says quickly. Then she turns to me. "Ready to go to work?"

My ears perk up.

You're doggone right I am!

Susan grabs her jacket and keys and gets me settled in her truck.

I've been doing my crisis-response work

for a while now. We get calls at all times of day—even in the middle of the night. Today, as we drive along, I pace back and forth. I wonder where we're headed. I wonder what the problem might be.

Will we be helping to soothe people after a scary event like an accident? Or a mudslide? Or something else?

I remember my first assignment, during a big wildfire in our state. Susan and I were sent to a camp where firefighters gathered to receive orders or to rest after fighting the blaze.

Whenever Susan saw a fire truck coming back to the camp, she would bring me out. As the exhausted men and women stepped from the truck, I'd be waiting, just in case anyone needed a furry friend. Lots of firefighters came over to pet me or talk to me. I could smell

the smoke on their gear. I could sense their weariness and sometimes their sadness. But even those tough and tired firefighters smiled when Susan gave them one of my trading cards. “This is great! I’ll give it to my son,” one man said to us. “My kid Jamie loves dogs.”

Yep—*Jamie*. The very same boy I met later in the classroom.

“And this is from our team to yours,” the man said to Susan. He gave us a pin from his firehouse! Susan wears it proudly on her cap now.

My thoughts about that wildfire are interrupted as Susan’s truck slows down. I peek out and see the familiar brown sign go by, and the ranger in the little building waving us through. We travel past sand and trees and hills. I can tell we’ve returned to the desert park.

But now, something has happened here. Someone needs us.

I may not know yet what the emergency is, but I know this: it's time to get to work.

Chapter 5

Searchers Assemble

Susan and I first meet up with my bloodhound friend, Bear, and his human, Christopher. As we wait for the others, Susan fastens my search and rescue vest on me. Soon we're joined by Birdie and Pilot with Marisol and RJ. All of us—humans and dogs—are wearing our matching yellow gear.

Now I know what the emergency must be.

Whenever our team gets called out together, it means one thing: someone is missing!

Although I'm training to do search work, I know I won't be sent out to find people. I'm here to help by using my skills as a crisis-response therapy dog.

Once our team is assembled, we travel to the command center where several park rangers are gathered. Some of the rangers are looking at maps. There's a radio set up on a picnic table.

To one side, there are two people who are not in uniform—a woman and a little girl sitting on camp chairs. They look worried.

A park ranger we've worked with before, Ranger Griffin, greets our team. "Thank you for coming out," he says. "I know you're all volunteers taking time from your busy lives. We truly appreciate the help."

Then he fills us in on the situation. "A sixteen-year-old boy named David is missing in the park. He was camping here with his family," Ranger Griffin explains. "We've talked with his mother. She told us David wants to be a photographer. He took the family car and set out at dawn. He planned a short hike to take nature photos, but he hasn't been seen since. David told his little sister, Penny, he'd be back

before breakfast. He didn't bring much food or water."

"His family must be so worried," Marisol says quietly. "It's nearly dinnertime."

"Yes," says Ranger Griffin. "His mother is afraid that he's lost or injured. Otherwise, he'd be back by now. And have you heard tonight's weather forecast?"

"Chilly tonight, with rain," Susan says.

Uh-oh, I think.

I see how worried Susan and the others look, and I know why. Mostly the desert here is hot and dry. But the weather can change quickly. Susan and I once narrowly escaped something called a *flash flood* that ripped through the park during a storm. Thick brown water poured from the rocky hills that day, crashing down to a place we'd been standing not long before.

"David didn't say where he was going, but we have a lead," Ranger Griffin continues. "We found the family car parked near a trailhead. We'll start the canines searching there."

Ranger Griffin glances toward the two people on a bench. "Understandably, David's family is pretty upset."

"Skye and I are here to help," Susan says. "We'll sit with the family as they wait for news."

Ranger Griffin nods. "While we set up a search plan with the rest of the team, Ranger Kay will introduce you," he says.

Ranger Kay steps forward and leads us toward the mom and the little girl.

Ranger Kay greets the family. "We're doing everything we can right now to find your son

and your brother," she tells them. "This is Susan, and this sweet dog is Skye. Skye is here to visit with you, if you'd like."

David's mom jumps up to shake hands with Susan. But the little girl, David's sister, Penny, holds back.

As Susan speaks with the mom, I see my friends get into vehicles with their humans and some of the rangers. I know they're heading out to begin the search.

Good luck, Bear, Birdie, and Pilot, I think as I watch the trucks pull away. *Please find that young man before it's too late!*

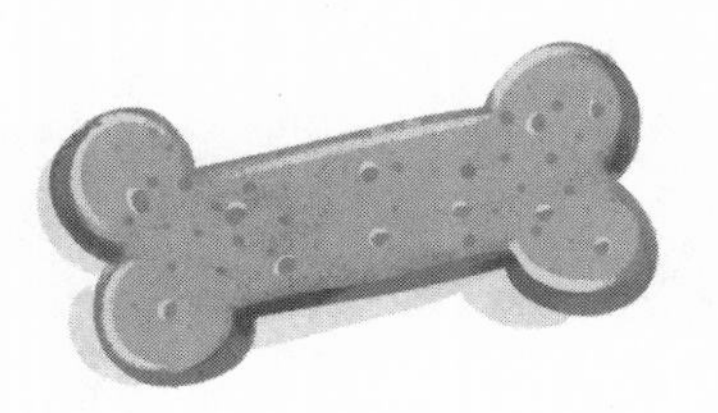

Chapter 6

A Clue

It doesn't take long for Penny to glance at me. "Hi, Skye," she says. "I like your friendly eyes."

I look up at her.

You have kind eyes too, I think. *And they're brown, like mine!*

But her eyes are a little red around the edges. I smell those salty, wet things humans call *tears*.

The little girl scooches closer. "Can I pet her?" she asks Susan.

"Of course," Susan says gently. "She's here for you today."

Penny rests her hand on my back. She doesn't speak much at first. Instead, she begins to hum a little song to me. I don't mind. Hanging out with me is helping steady her fears, I can tell. We stay like that for a while.

The sun sinks lower in the sky. That worries me a bit. We've done some training searches at night. Things are always harder in the dark. There are only a couple hours till sunset now. I hope my team members will have good news for this family soon.

For a long time, Penny pats me and hums her songs. Then she begins to speak in a soft voice. "I've been sad all day, Skye," she tells me. "You know why? My brother is lost."

Don't worry, Penny, I think. *My friends are on the job! And they're the best! They've found missing hikers before.*

"David left early this morning," Penny tells me as she ruffles my fur. "Mom was still asleep, but he said goodbye to me. David said he was going to take nature pictures. And he'd be back

to have breakfast with us. I saw him pack his water bottle and a granola bar in his backpack. I told Mom and the rangers all about that, so they can save him."

Penny relaxes more as we sit together. I hope sharing her thoughts with me makes her feel better. Then Penny begins to talk about something else.

"Skye, have you ever seen a real, live desert bighorn sheep?" Penny asks.

Those big, skittish critters with the curly horns? I think. *Sure I have! One jumped out and scared me once here in the park!*

"Well, I really like bighorn sheep," Penny says. She holds up a stuffed animal with curly horns for me to see.

Sweet! That looks like one of my doggy toys, I think.

"This is just a pretend bighorn sheep. I've never seen a real one," Penny says. "David told me he'd get a picture of a real one today. He knows a special place in the park where they go."

Penny's mom has been pacing, her footsteps crunching on the gravelly sand with each step. Suddenly, she stops.

"What's that honey?" she asks. "David planned to get photos of the bighorn sheep? Did he tell you that?"

Penny's eyes grow wide. "I just remembered," she said. "I didn't think about it until I started talking to Skye."

Penny's mother looks at Susan, and Susan nods. "There are a few places in the park where herds of desert bighorn sheep graze," she says. "Your son could have found information on the

park's website and headed that way. This could help guide our search."

Susan turns to the little girl. "Penny, Skye and I will be right back. What you just told Skye about David wanting to take a photo of a bighorn sheep—that's an important clue. And it just might help the rangers to find your brother."

Chapter 7

A New Mission

Susan brings me with her when she talks to Ranger Griffin. The ranger nods as he listens.

"That's a good lead," he says. "David might have been trying to reach Kestrel Ridge. We've been studying a herd of bighorn sheep there. But it's a long walk from where his car is parked. And there's a lot of rough terrain for someone who isn't an experienced hiker."

Ranger Griffin pauses, like he's thinking over the situation. "The other canines on your team set off on searches in other directions. I'll radio this information to them, but it would take a long time for any canine team to get to Kestrel Ridge, I'm afraid."

The ranger looks up at the darkening sky, then glances down at me. He hesitates.

"Unless you think..."

"That Skye and I could begin a search?" Susan asks quickly.

"I've seen how great your dog is with the family," Ranger Griffin says. "But is she ready for a mission like this?"

I look up at Susan. *Am I?*

"Skye's not search and rescue certified yet," Susan admits. "But that's on me. I wanted to be extra sure before getting her tested. She was a champ at trailing during training today, though," says Susan. "And if this young man, David, is hurt, the sooner we find him, the better."

"That's what I was thinking," Ranger Griffin agrees.

I watch the two humans as they talk. I can see the ranger is hopeful and Susan is nervous but eager.

"What do you think, Skye?" Susan says at last. "We can do this, can't we?"

I make a low, rumbly sound in agreement.

If it will help get David back with his family, I think, *then I really want to try!*

I guess Susan can read me pretty well. She looks at me and takes a deep breath. "Okay then," she says to Ranger Griffin. "We'll do it."

Before we leave the command center, though, there's something Susan has to take care of first. Together, we go back to David's family.

"I can tell that Skye liked meeting you, Penny," Susan says. "You spoke to her so kindly. But right now, we have to leave for a bit."

"Oh. Okay," says Penny. She doesn't look happy.

"Before we go, Skye and I want you to have something," Susan says. "It's our way of saying thank you for the nice visit today."

I see Susan pull something from her backpack. She hands one of my trading cards to Penny. “This card tells all about Skye, and it has her picture too,” Susan says. “It’s specially made for new friends she really likes, like you.”

When Penny looks down at the card, I catch sight of a change on her face.

For the first time since I’ve met her, the little girl smiles.

Chapter 8
Something in the Air

We leave Penny and her mom with Ranger Griffin and the others at the command center. It's hard to say goodbye. But I know we have important work to do. Ranger Kay volunteers to be our flanker, and the three of us load into Susan's truck. We drive to a turnoff down a small dirt road.

After we park, Susan brings me out and

grabs her backpack from the back seat. But we aren't ready to search yet. Quickly and carefully, Susan fits me with protective goggles and puts boots on my paws. I've tried on this stuff before but don't always wear it during training. I look like I mean business now, like

I'm a fearless search dog on a mission.

I hope I can live up to my image, I think.

Susan snaps a long leash to my collar, and we head over to a parked car.

"This is the car David drove here," says Ranger Kay. "We've checked out the license plate number his mom gave us. At least we know where he started from. But this is a big park, and David has been gone since morning.

There's no telling how far he has traveled on foot, especially if he got lost." She glances up. "And I don't like those storm clouds. We may be searching in the dark and the rain."

I may look the part of a search and rescue dog now, but I am worried too. I've proven myself as a therapy dog, helping to calm people during a crisis. But now I'm pretty jumpy myself. I'm not used to working out in the field, leading a search. What if I'm not good enough? What if I fail?

Then I think about Penny, worrying about her brother, and David's mom, upset about her son. I think of the hours Susan and I have spent honing our skills. I recall the confidence in Susan's voice as she praised me to Ranger Griffin. And I know I'm ready to try my best.

"David's mother gave us this," Ranger

Kay says. "It's from the T-shirt the teen wore yesterday."

Ranger Kay hands Susan a plastic bag with a scrap of material inside. I breathe in, and tuck that scent in my memory.

Check. Got it.

"All set, Skye?" Susan asks. Then she gives the command: "Search!"

I put my nose to the air. Other hikers have

traveled this way today, I can tell. There's car exhaust lingering in the air too. I can even smell traces of Bear, Birdie, Pilot, and their humans, who all started here and set off in different directions.

There's not a hint of David though.

Where is it? I think. *Where's the scent?*

When Susan sees that I'm not picking up the trail, she makes a decision.

"We'll start by moving toward Kestrel Ridge. If the young man read about the park's bighorn sheep and wanted a photo, that's where he would have headed," Susan says.

We set off quickly, with Ranger Kay close behind.

The ground is even at first. We wind through a landscape of rock, yucca, and prickly pear. All of these things have their own scent, but it's not the scent I'm looking for.

"Good job, Skye. Keep at it," Susan encourages me. And so I do.

The sun hovers above the horizon. It casts a golden glow but also throws dark shadows across the landscape. There's a change in the air too. It's cooler, and though it's not raining yet, I feel a hint of wetness in the wind.

"I hope he's found soon," Susan says as we hurry along. "I wouldn't want to stay outside on a chilly night like this."

Me neither, I think. *And I have a warm fur coat.*

We press on, heading for the rocky hills before us. I wonder if my teammates are having better luck.

"Do you think we're on the right track?" Ranger Kay asks.

RESCUE

"It's a good hunch that David went this way," Susan says. "But we can't be sure. Maybe he didn't read about Kestrel Ridge at all. Maybe he started off in another direction. Or maybe he got all the photos he wanted there and moved on. Right now, though, this is the best lead we have." Then she calls out to me, "Come on, Skye, we're counting on you."

I'm trying, Susan, I think. And I really am.

I breathe in all the desert smells and the distant rain. I smell a faraway scent I recognize as bighorn sheep.

I no longer smell Bear or Birdie or Pilot. Maybe they have already locked onto the right scent somewhere else. As we continue on, I'm hoping, for David's sake, that they have.

If I don't find the scent soon, will Susan and Ranger Kay still trust me? I wonder. *Will our search here be delayed so a more experienced dog can take over?*

We follow a curve in the path, and I pause. I'm ready to try again with everything I have.

I wiggle my nose, drawing in as much air as I can, looking for a match to the scent marked "David" in my memory. There's nothing at first. And then…

There! That's it!

In all the bits of smells floating in the desert tonight, I catch the tiniest whiff of a scent like the one on the T-shirt.

And then I know—David traveled this way, and he's out here.

Somewhere.

Chapter 9
Daring Rescue

"She's got it," Susan tells Ranger Kay. There's an edge of excitement in her voice. "She's found the scent."

"How can you tell?" Ranger Kay asks.

"Just watch her."

I sniff the air again, then turn my nose to the ground. Since it's cool, the scent isn't rising as it does in heat. I can smell it best near the dirt. As I trot along, the scent leads me off the path, and soon Susan and Ranger Kay and I are hurrying across the rocky land, making our way to the hills ahead.

A late-afternoon breeze is stirring things up, but I've got a hold on the scent, and I follow it along the ground. Then, suddenly, it's gone.

I lost it, I think. *No!*

I think back to the time I lost the scent during training. That morning, I got so excited about the hunt that I chased after the wrong smell. I won't make the same mistake again. I stop, plant my feet, and wiggle my head and shoulders. The movement shimmies down my whole body to my tail. I always feel better after a good doggy shake-off.

"It's okay, Skye," Susan says gently. She knows this move is my way of throwing off my frustration and starting fresh. "You'll find it again."

I hope so, I think. With my nose pointed in the air, I'm back to sniffing and seeking.

A raw, chilling wind begins to blow. In that gust, I catch another whiff of the bighorn sheep—and something else.

I'm off like a roadrunner, sprinting ahead on my long leash. I'm determined not to let the T-shirt scent get away from me again. I am so focused that Ranger Kay's sudden yell startles me.

"Rattler!" she cries out. "Right!"

I know what those words mean, and I skid to a stop. Then I see it. Ahead of us lies a snake with distinct, dark markings along its back. I look into the eyes of one of the deadliest animals of the desert and hear the rattling start.

SAR
RESCUE

I back away. *Whoa! That was too close!*

Susan sees the snake now too. She gasps and changes her course.

"Looks like a Mojave green rattler," Ranger Kay says as we make a wide detour around the snake. "Rare to see one out in this weather."

Rare or not, I'm glad Ranger Kay was paying attention. I do not have time to deal with a snakebite now. Not when there's someone I'm trying to save.

Luckily, the distraction hasn't caused me to lose the scent. It's still there, leading me to the bottom of a range of rocky hills. I'm reminded of today's trailing game. But no one pops down from atop a boulder this time, like Marisol did this morning.

Instead, we move forward. The scent is leading me upward.

Susan stops and pulls off her backpack. “Hold on, Skye,” she says. “Safety first.”

She gets on one knee and puts on her helmet. Then Susan, the ranger, and I begin picking our way up the rocky hill. It’s slow going at first. We have to scramble over rocks and watch our footing so we don’t slip.

The scent continues up and around the slope

we are climbing. We fight our way forward as the sky grows darker and the air gets colder.

Once we get a little higher, we come upon a flatter area. It's easier to run here. There's a rough path, maybe one that the bighorn sheep follow. David has come this way, too, I can tell. But just as I begin to pick up speed, I'm led right to the edge of a cliff. I stop before I get too close.

Uh-oh! A strong pool of scent rises to my nose from below.

Susan holds tightly to my leash and peers over the edge. "There's a ledge down there," she calls out to Ranger Kay. "I see a metal water bottle.

It could be David's. He may have fallen or slid over the edge. But…I don't see him."

"I know this area pretty well," Ranger Kay says. "If we keep going on this path, it circles around this hill and will lead us down there. We could go that way, but it may take an hour or more." She looks up at the darkening sky. "Or…"

"Or I could rappel down there with Skye to continue the search," Susan says. "I've got my climbing equipment in my backpack."

Did I mention that Susan, my amazing human partner, is a rock climber too?

Rappel is her fancy word for climbing down cliffs with rope.

After talking on the radio with the command center, Susan gets the go-ahead for a new plan. Ranger Kay will stay on the path above until

Susan and I rappel down to the ledge with a rope. If we find David, Ranger Kay will meet with other rescuers to help guide them to our location.

Susan reaches into her pack and lays out our climbing gear. My search and rescue vest comes off, and a special harness goes on. Susan fastens all the harness straps through the buckles, double-checking to make sure they're secure. She attaches a line to the top of the cliff; she will use that line to lower us down. Ranger Kay checks our equipment each step of the way.

Soon, Susan lowers us both over the edge. She holds on to the line with her shoes braced against the rock wall. I feel like one of the park's falcons, dangling in the air in my harness from a rope attached to my human.

We've climbed together like this before, during training. Luckily, heights don't bother me. I must be quite a sight, though, swinging in the sky this way.

Even before I'm lowered to the surface, the smell of scared human is so strong, it's almost overpowering. All of my instincts and all of my training kick in. My legs start pumping wildly even though I'm still hanging in the air.

Once my paws touch the ledge, I try to scramble to finish the job.

"Hold on, Skye," Susan says. She removes the line and my harness, fastens on my vest, and clips on my leash. Then, the minute she's done, she says the magic word: "Search."

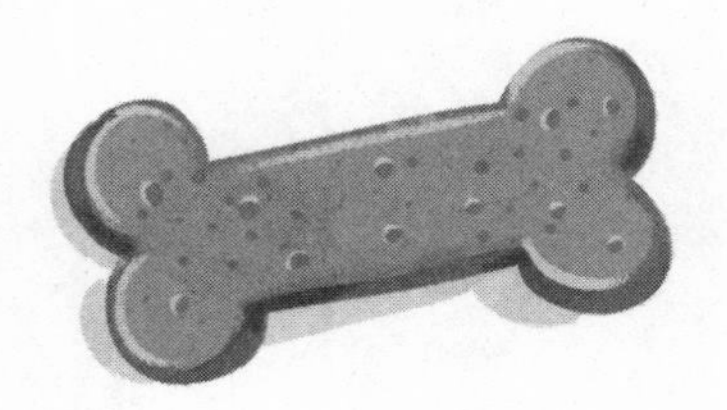

Chapter 10
Lost and Found

I bound ahead to a sheltered outcropping of rock. The scent grows stronger and stronger and stronger till—*bam!* It hits me like a wall.

Then I see two gym shoes sticking out from behind a boulder—and those shoes are attached to a human! I round the corner and see a teen boy lying on his back, shivering.

You don't look well, human, I think. But his

eyes are open wide when he turns and sees me. I know that's a good sign.

"You found him, Skye," Susan says as she catches up. "Oh, Skye! You wonderful, incredible, good dog! Good girl!" Susan slips me a treat. Then we move closer to the young man, who struggles to raise himself onto his elbows.

"No need to move," says Susan. "I'm with the park's volunteer canine search and rescue team. My name is Susan, and my dog here is Skye. Can you tell me your name, please?"

"I'm David. David Stevens," he answers. "I couldn't get a signal on my phone. I didn't know if anyone would find me."

"Well, Skye here found you. And I've got a warm blanket for you," Susan says, digging into her backpack. "Are you hurt, David?"

"I have a few cuts and some bruises, and I think my ankle is broken. I'm really thirsty. I slipped while taking pictures and sort of slid down the side of the cliff." He winces as he lowers himself back down. "It hurts to walk, but I pulled myself behind these rocks for shelter from the weather."

"I'm going to report to the command center

that we found you and request a medical team to help carry you out," says Susan. "Then is it okay if I check your ankle?"

Did I mention that Susan, my amazing human partner, is trained in wilderness first aid too?

Before the last of the sun slips away, Susan sets up a small light. I begin to hear the plop of water drops hitting stone. The rocks protect us from most of the rain, but some chilly droplets are carried in on the wind. In the distance, thunder rumbles.

Susan offers David water and a little food. She treats his cuts and looks at his ankle. She makes sure he's comfortable. And me? I'm having trouble sitting still after all the excitement.

But then I take a good look at David lying there, still frightened and in pain.

Can I help too? I wonder.

My instincts tell me I can. I snuggle close to David's side. As we wait for others to come up the path, David drops his hand and smooths the fur on my neck. I can feel the panic he's been fighting all day begin to melt away.

"So this dog helped find me?" he asks as lightning flashes in the night. "Thank you, Skye."

"Yes, she followed a scent trail right to you,"

Susan says. "Skye thinks it's the best game in the world."

"What a smart dog," David says. I give him a long look and wag my tail.

"I agree. And a determined one too," Susan says. "So your mom and your sister said you were going to take nature photos. Any success today?"

I can guess what Susan is doing. She's trying to keep David calm, too, in her own, human way. If she keeps David talking, maybe he won't think about the pain in his ankle.

"You met my mom and Penny?" David asks.

"Yes, back at the park's command center. Penny told us you wanted to take pictures of the bighorn sheep. That helped us a lot. That's why Skye and I were sent to search around Kestrel Ridge."

"Yeah," David admits. "I was looking for the herd that lives here. But the hike was harder than I thought. I got some good photos of wildflowers and even a desert iguana. But not the bighorn sheep I promised Penny."

"Trust me, she's not going to be disappointed," says Susan. "That little girl is just going to be happy to have her big brother safely back."

Finally, just as the thunder quiets and the rains slow, we are joined by Ranger Kay and a few other humans, who check David's foot and carefully settle him into a board called a *rescue stretcher*.

The crew carries David down the slippery hill. Susan and I follow as they bring him to a waiting ambulance. David's mom and Penny are there to meet him. I see David's mom squeeze his hand just before he's lifted into the

ambulance. Penny looks sleepy but happy. She waves to me before she and her mom climb into a car that follows the ambulance.

I allow myself a moment for another refreshing doggy shake-off. I steady my paws on the ground and wiggle away the excitement of the hunt, the worry that I'd fail, and all the fear I felt stirring in David. Let me tell you, letting it all go feels great.

By the time Susan and I return to the command center, the rest of our team is there to greet us. Someone hands Susan a cup of steaming tea, while I get some refreshing, cool water.

Ranger Griffin steps over to congratulate our team on a successful find. "We've heard from the hospital staff that David has a couple broken bones, but he's expected to make a full

recovery. You know the news reporters will be calling about this," he says. "Everyone loves a good story about a hero dog."

"Right," says Susan, "but our team has an agreement. We don't report to the media that one dog made the find. We announce that our *team* made a rescue. After all, each dog and each person plays a part in the search. As we see it, the success of one dog and handler is a win for our whole team."

"I get that," Ranger Griffins says.

Then all the rangers clap for us while Ranger Griffin shakes the hands of Susan, Christopher, Marisol, and RJ and pats me, Bear, Birdie, and Pilot on our heads.

Just before Susan goes to log tonight's mission details, she crouches next to me. "I guess it's time, Skye," she says. "There's no doubt you're ready to become a true, certified search and rescue dog. Sorry I waited so long. You sure proved yourself tonight." Then she kisses the top of my head.

At that moment, I think back to how people once saw me as the troublesome dog with bad habits and too much energy. I've come a long way since then. Now, I have two important jobs, and I get to do them both with my best friend, Susan.

It's been a long journey to get here, it's true. But along the way, I discovered this—in learning to find others, I think I've finally found all the best things about myself.

RESCUE

About SAR Dogs

The first search and rescue (SAR) dogs helped locate lost travelers in the mountains of Europe during the 1700s. Since then human's best friend has stepped up to help in all kinds of places and situations, from finding hurt soldiers on battlefields to locating people trapped in rubble after natural disasters.

While the goal of every SAR mission is similar, different kinds of searches may call for dogs with different skills and training. In the wilderness, teams need to cover huge areas, and every minute counts. If the searchers have an idea of where the missing person may be, they may use air-scent dogs. These dogs are trained to look for "pools" of scent, or places where a scent is strongest. So if there is a defined area to search, air-scent dogs are great at sniffing out the nearest humans.

But what if no one knows where the missing person may have gone? This is a job for a trailing dog, like Skye. Instead of looking for the strongest scent in an area, a trailing dog searches for a *particular* scent. Starting at the person's last known position, the dog takes a big whiff of the missing person's scent from things like clothing or personal belongings. Then it's on to the trail.

The trail the dog follows is not a visible path. Instead, it's a scent trail. A SAR dog can detect bits of the scent that may be drifting in the air, caught in branches, settled in the dirt, or even present in footprints. Humans shed about 40,000 skin cells per minute. That's a lot of skin! And while shedding skin may sound gross, it's just what SAR dogs need to be able to trail a missing person.

Still, the job isn't easy. Wind and heat and rain can all affect a dog's ability to stay on a scent trail. Not only that, after hours of sniffing, a dog's nose can become used to a particular scent, making it harder for the dog to follow. When this "nose fatigue" sets in, the dog needs to take a break and reset—and maybe give a good shake to de-stress, like Skye does. Then it's back on the job, following a trail that humans cannot see and bringing help to those in need.

What It Takes

Most SAR groups are made up of volunteers. But that doesn't mean that every team is not expertly trained. Each team—human and dog—spends hundreds of hours to become certified. For humans, this involves learning first aid (on both humans and dogs) as well as CPR. Humans may also be required to take classes in incident management, backcountry survival, and other skills specific to a certain area, such as rock climbing.

For dogs, training begins with the basics. All SAR dogs must have excellent obedience skills, be comfortable around humans, and have a strong hunting drive. To become certified with some SAR organizations, dogs need to complete a test where they follow a scent through the wilderness—for one full mile!

It takes a tough pup to do SAR work. Terrain is often rugged, and in deserts, like the one where Skye works, temperatures can reach 100°F by midmorning. It's important that humans and their dogs take every safety precaution so they can live long and healthy lives, doing the vital work that they do best.

SAR Dogs in This Book

Border Collie

This breed got its name from its job of herding sheep along the border of Scotland and England. Today the border collie is still the top herder in the world, but its smarts make it a great fit for other jobs too.

Height: 18–22 inches
Weight: 30–55 pounds
Life Span: 12–15 years
Coat: White and black or brown
Known for: Intelligence, energy

Bloodhound

Often owned by royalty in medieval times, this breed got its name because it was said to have "royal blood." Today it's known for having the best nose of any breed.

Height: 23–27 inches
Weight: 80–110 pounds
Life Span: 10–12 years
Coat: Black and tan, red
Known for: Independence, curiosity, friendliness

Breed information based on American Kennel Club data. For more on these and other breeds, visit www.akc.org/dog-breeds/.

Acknowledgments

Early one February morning, I took part in a most memorable adventure in California's Joshua Tree National Park. I accompanied a canine search and rescue team and witnessed their amazing training exercises in the beautiful desert setting. Many thanks to all present that day: Laura Finlon and Matt Finlon with their golden retrievers, Pippin and Gunner; Katy Priest with her goldendoodle, Dudley; and Robin Balch with her standard poodle, Laine. Much appreciation to Katy Priest for granting me a follow-up interview and providing photos of crisis-response dogs in action. An extra-special thank-you to Laura Finlon for answering my many questions, sending photos of Pippin in rappelling gear, and commenting on an early draft. Finally, much gratitude to the Albert Whitman team, my encouraging and inspiring editor Jonathan Westmark, and illustrator Francesca Rosa for the engaging scenes of Skye and the striking desert landscape.

Although this book is set in a fictional desert park, and Kestrel Ridge is a fictional location, some details were inspired by the natural features of Joshua Tree National Park.